Spy to Invade

Written by Steve Cole
Illustrated by Marina Halak

Collins

1 Mystery on the roof

All stories start somewhere. I guess this one started when Mum and I moved into the Tower in the middle of Caracas, in Venezuela. I'm Andrea by the way. Andrea Rivas.

The Tower is an unfinished skyscraper that stands forty-five storeys above the city streets. It was meant to be an office building, but the money ran out and it was never completed. Affordable homes are hard to find in Caracas, so people started moving into the Tower without permission. It's OK here. Most of us have electricity and we take it in turns to clean the corridors. Although we're not really allowed to be here, there's quite a nice community.

But when the other kids at school found out where I lived, they called me names: "Squatter! Space invader!"

I told Mum when I got back to our little apartment on the twenty-seventh floor. Most of the walls are made of wood and the one window is cracked.

"Is that why they call us space invaders?" I asked. "'Cos this space doesn't really belong to us?"

"It doesn't belong to anyone," Mum explained. "No one was using it. Now thousands of us are here! So many, the police leave us alone; they don't need the hassle. And if the police don't mind, why should your friends?" Mum placed a kiss on my forehead. "It's safer to live here than on the streets."

What I like about the Tower is that I can always see my home. Whether I'm at school or in the park or at the shops, it stands higher than anything else. People only live on the first twenty-eight floors. The seventeen floors above have no outer walls and there's no wiring for the electricity. There's just the stairwell that leads all the way up to the empty roof where helicopters were supposed to land.

One day, after school, I saw something weird had appeared on that roof. Something enormous, hidden by cream tarpaulin. It looked like it had dropped out of the sky.

When I got to the Tower lobby, I saw my mate Gabriel from the fifteenth floor riding his bike. "Hey!" I called to him. "Have you seen that strange thing on the roof?"

Gabriel shook his head. "What strange thing?"

"Come with me," I told him.

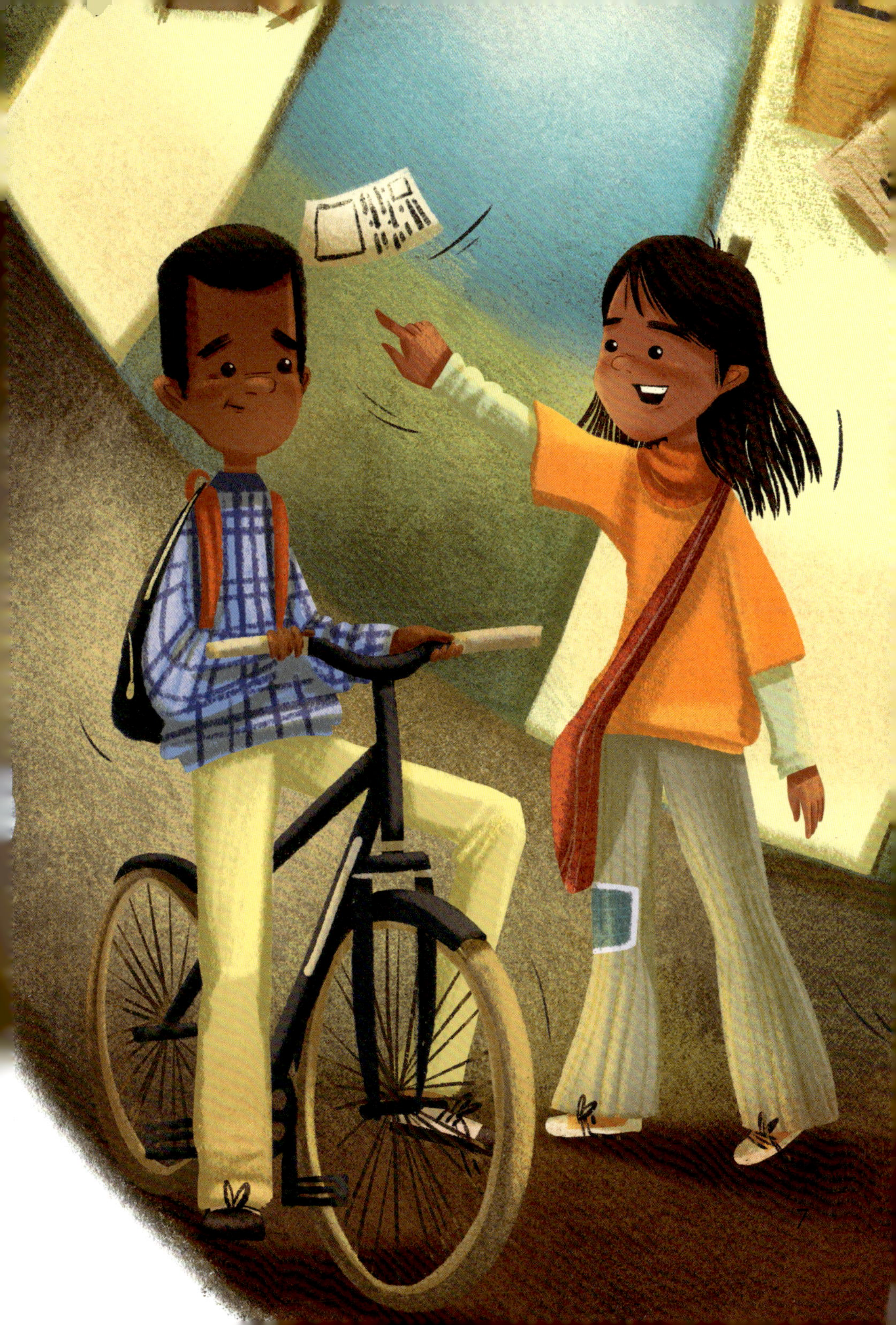

We took the stairs all the way up to the twenty-eighth floor. Because no one lives above the twenty-eighth floor, the stairs that go higher are very dusty and dirty.

The higher we got, the bigger the breeze down the stairwell into our faces. I was sweating and trying not to pant for breath.

Finally, we came out onto the roof. Sometimes people come up here to burn their rubbish or have secret parties. The helipad is built in the middle of the roof. Of course, no helicopter has ever really landed there.

The Mystery Thing on top of the helipad was huge. Beneath the cream sheets, it looked to be shaped like a giant upturned dish.

"Look." Gabriel pointed to graffiti on the wall: numbers and squiggles over the brickwork. Someone had drawn a large circle with twelve markings around it, like a clock face that told some secret sort of time.

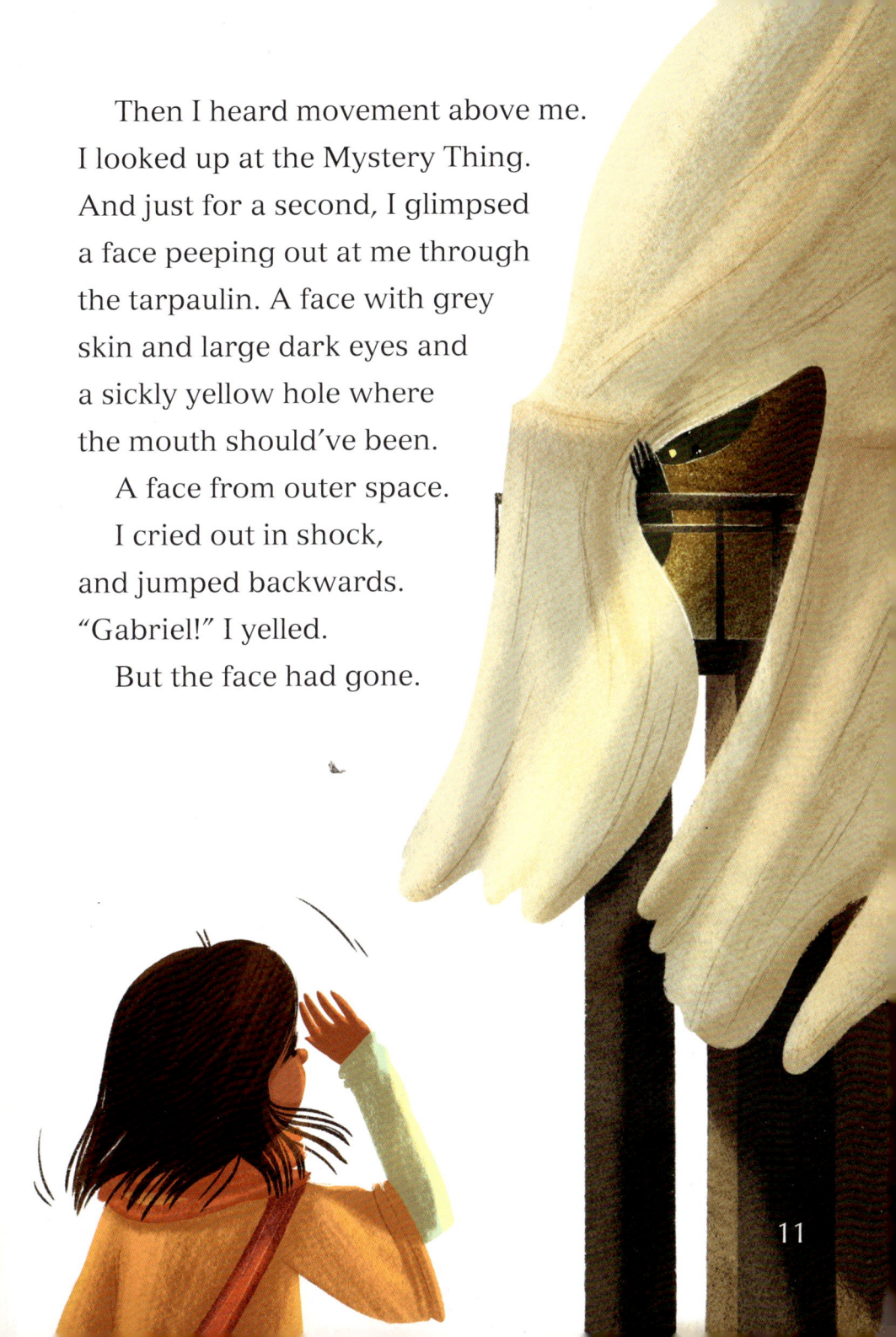

Then I heard movement above me. I looked up at the Mystery Thing. And just for a second, I glimpsed a face peeping out at me through the tarpaulin. A face with grey skin and large dark eyes and a sickly yellow hole where the mouth should've been.

A face from outer space.

I cried out in shock, and jumped backwards. "Gabriel!" I yelled.

But the face had gone.

2 The girl from the shadows

"What's up with you, Andrea?" Gabriel demanded.

"I saw something behind the tarpaulin," I told him. "A super-creepy alien face!"

"Right." Gabriel smirked. "Think I'm gonna fall for that?"

"It's true!" I insisted. Feeling scared and angry, I headed back to the stairs. "Mum's expecting me back. Let's go."

I left Gabriel at the twenty-seventh floor and he carried on down to his place on the fifteenth. I stepped out into my corridor. I could hear Mum's music, and smell the chicken soup she was cooking – familiar and comforting.

Then someone stepped into sight from the shadows at the end of the corridor. It was a girl, about my age. Someone I'd never seen before. Her eyes were wide and dark.

"Hi," I said. "I haven't seen you around before."

"We are just passing through," the girl said, and pointed to the ceiling. She had a foreign accent I didn't recognise. "We come from up there. My name is Vega."

"I'm Andrea." Feeling uneasy, I crossed to my front door.

"You should stay away from the roof, Andrea," Vega called. "It is not safe."

I turned to look at her. But she'd gone.

With a shiver, I opened my door and went inside.

Mum blew me a kiss but she was scowling as usual. "What time d'you call this? You want me to do all the work myself? Come and help with the soup!"

I smiled, glad that something felt normal today.

After dinner, I did some homework and then I went to my "room" – a mattress on the floor with a with a screen next to it. Mum argued with Aunt Paola on the phone for ages. Normally I hate their rows, but that night I was glad of the distraction.

I was trying not to think of the grey face with the big dark eyes. Kids at school called *me* a "space invader" – but, up on the roof, had I seen the real thing?

I couldn't concentrate through school the next day. On my way home through the noisy city streets, I looked up at the Tower. The sheets were still shrouding whatever clung to the top.

"Hey! Andrea."

The voice made me jump. It was Gabriel on his bike, beckoning urgently.

I joined him. "What's up?"

"I'm trailing someone." Gabriel pointed across the street. "Keep watching the alleyway. She'll come out in a minute."

Sure enough, a figure emerged from the quiet alley, and I felt a chill. It was creepy Vega from last night. She was carrying a big holdall on her back.

"There's an empty old book shop down there," Gabriel informed me. "Vega just went up the fire escape."

I frowned. "How'd you know her name?"

"She was waiting outside my door last night," said Gabriel. "Warned me to stay away from the roof."

"Same," I told him, rubbing my arms to get rid of my goosebumps.

"It sounded like she was up to something," said Gabriel. "So, when I saw Vega leaving the Tower this morning, I thought I'd follow her. That's the fifth place she's been to today." He pulled a face. "I trailed her to an old hotel in Altamira … an old water tower in Estado Leal … a park in El Conde – "

"Sounds like the worst tour of Caracas ever," I said, setting off down the street. "Come on, let's see where she goes next!"

Vega was easy to spot along Lecuna Avenue, with her blonde hair and holdall. She moved slowly and carefully and barely looked up from her phone, like she was following a map.

Finally, Vega turned down a side street near the Miranda Plaza and climbed another fire escape. She looked around to check nobody was watching her, placed something on the windowsill and then vanished.

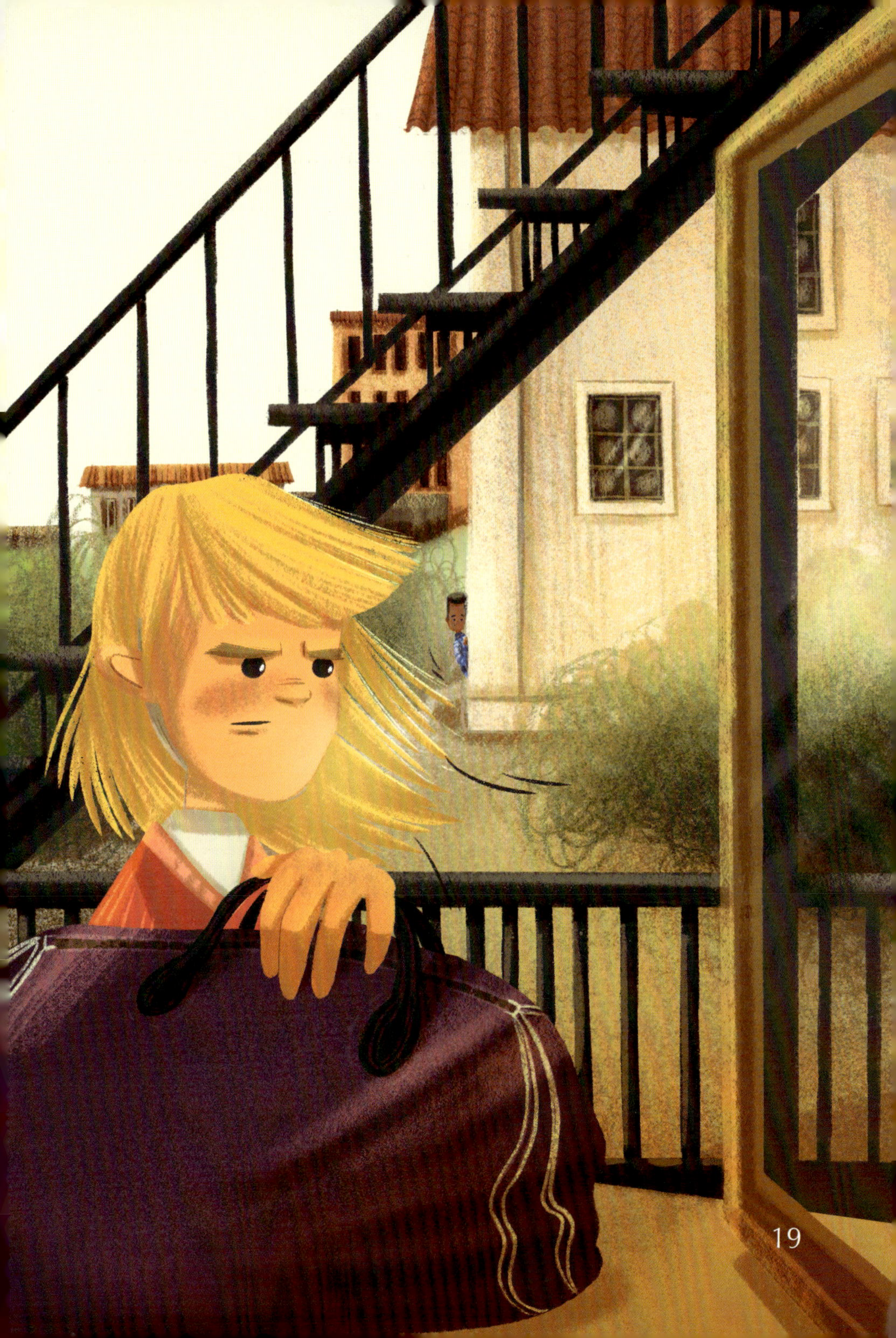

"What is she doing?" hissed Gabriel. "And what did she put up there?"

"I don't know," I said, nervous. "Should we go after her? She could be in trouble."

Gabriel hid his bike behind some empty rubbish bins. With a deep breath, I led the way up the fire escape. There was a staircase dead ahead. To our right was a huge storeroom loaded with rotting rolls of carpet. Rats scuttled in the gloom.

We nervously climbed the metal steps to the second floor, trying not to make any noise. Vega was nowhere to be seen.

A weird electronic hum started up on the second-floor windowsill and a blue-green glow filled the air around them.

"Quickly, in here!" I grabbed Gabriel's arm and pulled him back from the blue-green glow.

The hum faded. There was a clatter of footsteps on the fire escape below us. I saw Vega's face staring up at me and held my breath. She lingered as if trying to decide what to do. Then she ran off.

It was a few seconds more before I dared to release my breath. "OK, let's have a look at what's making that glow," I said.

Gabriel followed a step behind as we climbed up towards it.

"What's that?" I murmured, and had a closer look. The box was humming – like the sound from earlier with the volume right down. There was a weird gadget inside: a kind of turquoise oval with two little aerials slowly turning in the eerie luminous glow. There were squiggles on the oval – like the squiggles I'd seen last night on the Tower roof.

"Why would Vega leave *that* here?" Gabriel stared. "What is it, anyway?"

"It's alien," I breathed. "And I bet Vega's an alien too!"

3 Danger closing in

"Not this alien stuff again!" Gabriel groaned. "Chill, Andrea! It was someone pranking you in a mask last night, that's all."

"Yeah? And Vega just made that blue-green glow with her phone, did she?" I stared down at the glowing oval device. "What *is* this thing? Why would she bring it all the way here and leave it?"

"I dunno. She might have left one in every place she's been to." Gabriel took a picture of the oval on his phone, then closed the box. "Should we tell the police about this?"

"Oh, sure," I said, with sarcasm, "and tell them that two kids from the biggest slum in the city were following our neighbour all day because she was putting boxes on windowsills."

"You're right," said Gabriel. "We'll tell Mr Molina about it."

Mr Molina is like our mayor. He says who can live in the Tower and who can't, because not everyone who wants to live there is nice and he wants to make it as safe as possible.

We crept out of the building and Gabriel got his bike and we took turns to cycle back to the Tower.

When we reached the lobby, I saw my mum. She was struggling with shopping bags and yelling down the phone at Aunt Paola again.

"Andrea!" She waved at the bags crossly. "A little help, here, please!"

I looked at Gabriel. "Wait for me before you tell Mr Molina. I'll be back down as soon as I can."

Gabriel nodded and held up his phone to show me the picture of Vega's weird gadget. "Can't wait to see what he makes of this."

"*Andrea!*" Mum yelled.

I was glad Mum was too busy grouching at Aunt Paola to ask about my day on the way to our apartment. My stomach was fizzing at the thought of telling Mr Molina about Vega and what we'd seen. No sooner had Mum got the shopping through the front door than I was waving bye and racing all the way back down to the lobby.

I'd been away for less than 15 minutes in total. *Not bad,* I thought proudly.

Gabriel was riding his bike down the hallway. He waved as he saw me run up to him. "Hey, Andrea! Long time no see."

"What are you on about?" I frowned. "Come on, let's find Mr Molina."

Gabriel's face was blank. "Why?"

I frowned. "What, you forgot we just spent an hour following Vega?"

"Who's Vega?" he said.

"This isn't funny." I swiped his phone from his pocket, ignoring his protests as he climbed off his bike. "I suppose you don't remember the picture you took of that glowing thing – ?"

But the photo wasn't there.

"Are you crazy?" Gabriel grabbed his phone back. "I haven't seen you since yesterday, Andrea!"

Angry and afraid, I turned away from him. Across the lobby, I saw Vega standing with a man – her father, perhaps? They were watching me. Unsmiling. Unblinking.

My cheeks were burning, but I pretended not to notice the two figures as I hurried back to the staircase. My legs were aching like crazy, but I was so scared that Vega and her creepy dad would follow me, I ran the first three flights.

Only once I was sure I wasn't being followed did I trudge the rest of the way back up to the twenty-seventh floor.

My mind felt full of flies. What had happened to Gabriel to make him forget? Would something happen to me too?

I got my answer when I was about to push open the stairwell door to my corridor. It was wedged open a crack, and through the gap, I saw someone standing outside my apartment.

It was a woman. A woman who looked like Vega, right down to the staring, unblinking eyes. Her neck was kind of baggy, like a bullfrog's. I felt sick as she pulled the skin tight, and then tucked it into the neckline of her top.

She's wearing a mask, I realised. *What does she look like underneath?*

I could guess.

Beneath that mask, I just knew her skin would be grey … her eyes big and black … her mouth a gaping yellow hole.

I turned from the door and hurried on up the stairs to the roof.

What could I do now, by myself?

I'll just have to try and find more evidence, I decided. If I could show my mum and Mr Molina, they'd be able to do something. They'd keep me safe.

Wouldn't they?

Lost in thought, at last I pushed open the door to the roof. Night had fallen, and Caracas buzzed and blazed with a million lights. I looked out at the skyscraper canyons of stone and steel and felt so alone.

I turned and stared up at the helipad, and the tarpaulins flapping in the breeze. Then I noticed the circle etched into the helipad's wall – and I saw, for sure, that the drawing at "five o'clock" on the circle matched the mark on the glowing turquoise oval.

Suddenly, I heard movement behind me. I darted for the cover of a nearby pile of wood, just as Vega stepped through the door with her dad.

The man walked up to the circle on the wall. "You have placed the devices where we marked them on the map?"

"Yes," said Vega. "The devices are prepared. Once the human is mind-wiped like her friend, we can move to the next stage."

They're talking about me, I thought with horror. *That's why the woman was waiting at my door – to make me forget!*

Then I saw something that chilled both blood and bones. The man put his hands to his neck and pulled off his human disguise – revealing grey skin and dark alien eyes.

With an inhuman leap, he jumped up onto the roof of the heliport and ducked under the tarpaulin. The huge Mystery Thing glowed for a few moments.

It was shaped like an enormous metal saucer supported by four struts.

It could only be the aliens' spacecraft!

That thing didn't fall out of the sky, I realised. *It* landed *here*!

4 Hunted

As Vega walked across the roof towards the spaceship, I circled round the pile of wood and dashed for the stairwell. I slipped through the door and tried to take the steps as quietly as I could, but my legs were stiff from charging up and down and back up the stairwell. I gritted my teeth and forced myself to keep going. I had to get down to the lobby and warn Mr Molina. He could make the police listen and help us …

Couldn't he?

As I neared the twenty-eighth floor, a deep iron squeak cut the darkness. It was the stairwell door from the floor below being pushed open.

I held myself as still as a statue, afraid of what might hear me.

"We know that you know about us, Andrea," the female voice called up from the darkness. "Don't be afraid. We can make you forget everything."

It's Vega's mother. I closed my eyes. *The space invader.*

I tried to shrink smaller into the shadows as footsteps, slow and deliberate, started up the stairs.

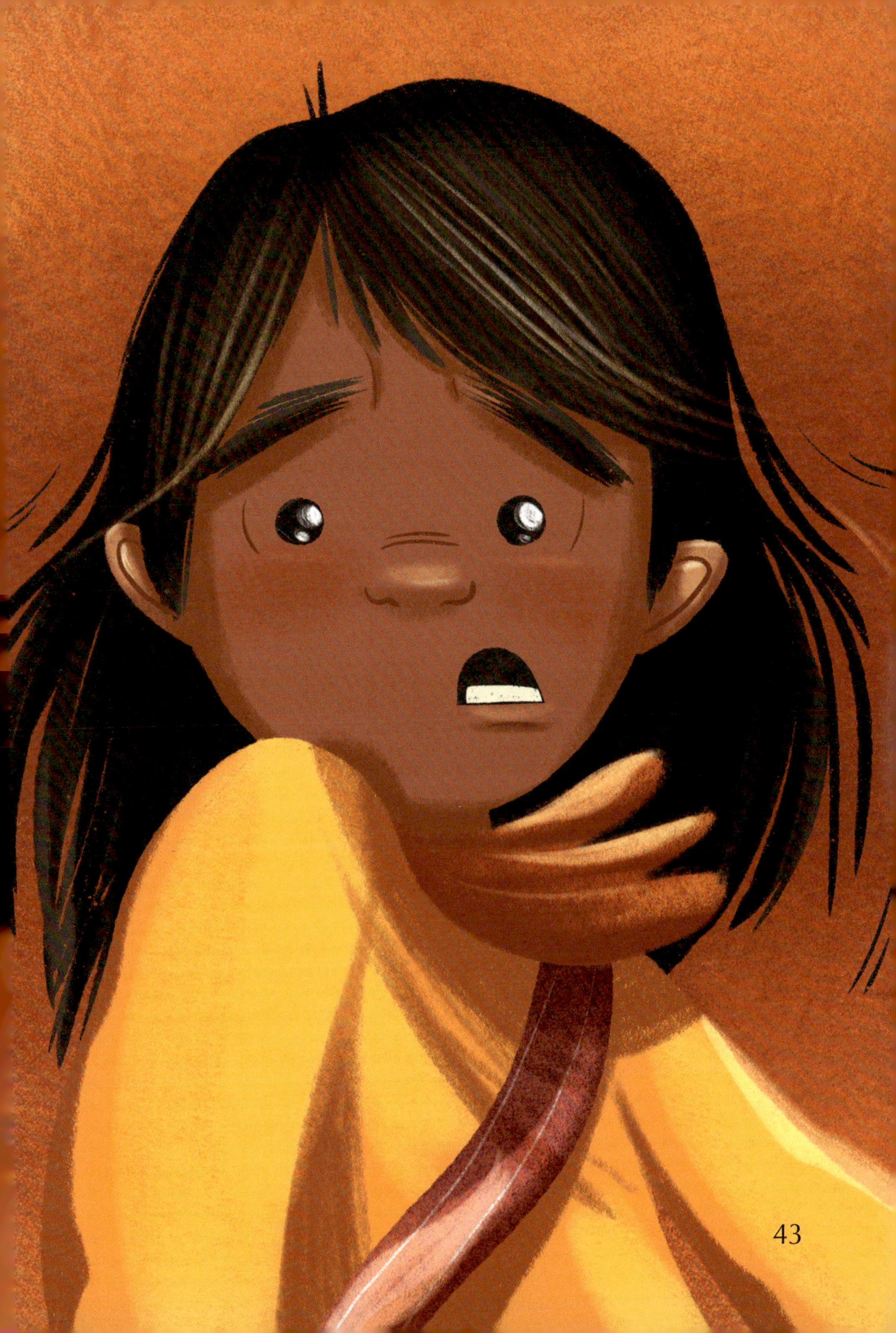

"I'm coming to find you," the woman said.

Terrified, I broke cover and made a run for it. I hit the ground running as I took the next flight of stairs down. Ahead, I saw Vega's mother blocking my way.

She lunged for me, but I ducked under her arms and kept going. I ran so fast I bounced off the walls of the stairwell as I turned the corners. But I was too frightened to feel the bruises.

"Help!" I wailed, but there was no one around. Normally loads of people hung out on the stairs. What had the aliens done with them?

We're all being made to forget, I thought, so these things *can do whatever they want.*

I burst out into the lobby. No one was there. But I could hear footsteps somewhere behind me.

The aliens were coming.

And so, again, I broke into a run. I pelted clear out of the lobby, through the parking garage and out into the streets.

I kept looking back over my shoulder, checking for any sign of Vega or her family. There was only one thing I could think to do that might stop them.

Everything depended on how fast I could reach the glowing device we found.

I didn't dare ask passers-by for help. Even if I'd had time, in the eyes of others, I was a no-good freeloader kid from the skyscraper slum – a trickster or a liar. Who cared what happened to the sort of people who lived in the Tower? Suspicious eyes followed me as I ran through the avenues, and strangers stared from shop doorways. They probably thought I'd stolen something to be racing away so fast. But I hadn't stolen anything.

Finally, I reached the old fire escape. My whole body shook for air as I staggered up the fire escape to the windowsill where the little box stood.

I grabbed the box and ran back down the steps.

There was the glowing turquoise oval. Its blue-green light tingled my skin as I cupped it carefully in my hands.

There was a noise behind me, and I turned.

Vega and her parents were standing in the street behind me.

"Put that down, Andrea," said Vega's mum.

"No!" I panted. "Stay back or I'll smash it into a million pieces."

Vega's dad stepped closer. "You must not do that."

"If you destroy the device, we cannot leave," said Vega. "And leaving is all we want to do."

I stared at her. "What?"

"We come from space," Vega said. "But we are no more space invaders than you are."

Vega's dad nodded. "I expect you and your mother came to the Tower because it is safer than the space around it. We came to Earth for the same reasons."

"Our ship ran out of power," Vega explained. "We had to land and recharge somewhere high above the ground so we could launch safely back into space." She pointed to the oval in my hands. "We have placed twelve special shock-swallowers in a protective ring around the Tower. When we blast off, they will absorb the shockwaves."

I stared into her unblinking eyes. "Seriously?"

"Yes," said Vega's mum. "Without them, every building for kilometres around will be flattened.

"Please, Andrea." Vega pulled off her mask and revealed her grey, alien face. She held out her hands and smiled. "Give me that shock-swallower?"

I looked into her dark eyes. I thought of all the nasty looks I'd been given because of where I came from. But I knew I was a good person, whatever some people thought.

"Here." With shaking hands, I handed Vega the glowing oval. "Take it."

"Thank you," she whispered, and placed it back in the box. "Thank you for trusting us."

Gabriel would have trusted you too," I said. "You didn't have to make him forget."

"It is better that no human suspects the truth of us," said Vega's dad.

"But we will trust you to keep our secret." Vega pulled her human mask back on. "We are ready to leave now. Perhaps one day we will return, Andrea. Then, you will know us again."

Without another word, the three aliens turned and left. Exhausted and aching all over, I took a long, deep breath and drank in the city air. I stayed for an hour or more, getting back my breath.

All the time, I stared across at the Tower.
The alien craft on top was glowing like a night light.
Suddenly it changed from soft white to fierce orange.
The box rattled behind me and burst into brilliant
flames as the shock-swallower helped absorb
the effects of the spaceship taking off. I gasped,
staring as the blazing oval swallowed itself whole to
leave nothing behind …

And when I looked back at the Tower, its roof
stood dark and empty. The spaceship had gone.

The aliens had kept their word. They'd left us and
kept the city safe. The shock-swallower had
vanished, too.

From then on, life went on a lot like before. Mum argued with Aunt Paola, I hung out with Gabriel and went to school each day. And still, at school or in the streets around the Tower, I heard the insults – "Dirty space invader!"

But I just smiled to myself.

Because one thing I know: sticks and stones may break my bones – but space invaders won't hurt me.

Dear Diary,

I've been thinking about me and Vega – different kinds of space invaders. And I'm trying to list what we have in common.

Vega has her mum and dad. I have my mum and Gabriel.

Vega was taken to the Tower because she had nowhere safe to go. Mum took me to the Tower because she had nowhere safe to go.

Vega didn't think anyone would trust her because of where she came from. I wonder if anyone will ever trust me because of where I come from.

Vega's skin colour is different to mine because her background is different, but we're still just people.

I'm thinking about her. I wonder if she's thinking about me?

55

Ideas for reading

Written by Gill Matthews
Primary Literacy Consultant

Reading objectives:
- check that the book makes sense to them, discussing their understanding and exploring the meaning of words in context
- ask questions to improve their understanding
- draw inferences such as inferring characters' feelings, thoughts and motives from their actions, and justify inferences with evidence
- predict what might happen from details stated and implied

Spoken language objectives:
- ask relevant questions to extend their understanding and knowledge
- articulate and justify answers, arguments and opinions
- participate in discussions, presentations, performances, role play, improvisations and debates

Curriculum links: Relationships Education – Families and people who care for me; Caring friendships; Respectful relationships

Interest words: sarcasm, grouching, protests, trudge

Resources: paper, pencils, computer

Build a context for reading

- Ask children to look closely at the front cover of the book. Explore what the title means to them.
- Read the back-cover blurb. Ask children why they think the aliens might have come.
- Ask children what kind of book they think this is. Discuss other science-fiction stories they've read and what features they expect this story to have.

Understand and apply reading strategies

- Read pp2–11 aloud, using appropriate expression. Discuss children's reaction to this first chapter. Check that children understand why Andrea and her mum live in the Tower.
- Ask children what they think the thing on the roof is. Encourage them to support their responses with reasons and evidence from the text.
- Encourage children to predict what might happen next in the story.